For my inspiring children—J. S.

For my brother and Vania—B. N.

First published in the United States by
Dial Books for Young Readers
A division of Penguin Putnam Inc.
345 Hudson Street
New York, New York 10014

Published in Great Britain by Macmillan Children's Books
Text copyright © 1999 by Jonathan Shipton
Pictures copyright © 1999 by Barbara Nascimbeni
All rights reserved • Typography by Pamela Darcy

Printed in Belgium on acid-free paper
First Edition
1 3 5 7 9 10 8 6 4 2

Library of Congress Cataloging in Publication Data
Shipton, Jonathan.
What if?/by Jonathan Shipton; pictures by Barbara Nascimbeni.—1st ed.
p. cm.
Summary: A young boy imagines an adventure among the clouds with an amazing girl
named Arabella, who encourages him to try things he has never done.
ISBN 0-8037-2390-3 (trade)
[1. Imagination—Fiction.] I. Nascimbeni, Barbara, ill. II. Title.
PZ7.S5576Wh 1999 [E]—dc21 98-33894 CIP AC

The art was created using acrylic paint and collage media.

What if?

by Jonathan Shipton

pictures by
barbara nascimbeni

Dial Books for Young Readers New York

What if . . .
it stopped raining?

What if it stopped raining
and you went outside,
and down at the end
of the garden
you found . . .

a sunflower as tall
as a skyscraper!

What if you
were a really
good climber, and
up you went, quick
as a monkey,

hand over hand,
leaf by leaf,

until you were up as high
as the highest chimney!

What if you kept on climbing until you were higher than a bird can fly . . .

until your head popped through the clouds!

but this girl is AMAZING!

Her name is Arabella
and she knows how
to leapfrog
on clouds.

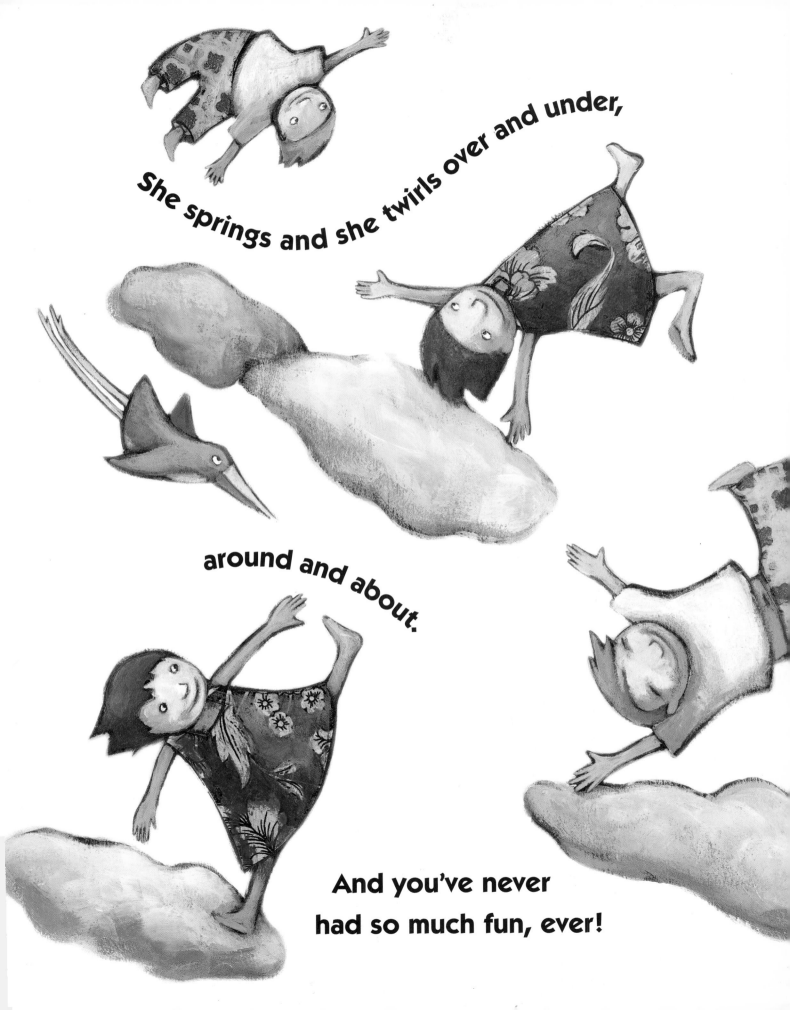

She springs and she twirls over and under,

around and about.

And you've never had so much fun, ever!

Then what if
Arabella says she
knows where storms begin . . .
and she takes you there . . .
where lightning flashes and
dark clouds rumble over
mountains to the sea.

What if you say it's
kind of scary . . .

and Arabella says
it's an adventure!
But what if you get
REALLY SOAKING WET . . .

and you and Arabella have to float
over the desert to drip-dry your clothes,
and the drips drop on camels.

What if it gets hotter . . .
and
hotter . . .
and
hotter . . .

and suddenly your cloud starts melting away!

So you head for home, quick
as you can, and Arabella
shows you how to

flap your arms to go faster!

But you screech
to a stop just in
time, when you see
your sunflower
popping its
head through
the clouds.

But what if
it still
looks a long
way away,
and you're
too scared
to jump?
But Arabella
says, "You
can do it!
You can do
ANYTHING
if you try!"

So you jump.
And it's the
best jump
you've
ever
done!

And as you fly through the sky, you can hear
Arabella clapping and cheering.

Down you go,
leaf by leaf,
just like a monkey.

Down and **down** and **down,** all the way to the good old solid ground!

But what if you landed on a secret door . . .

and behind it THERE WERE STEPS . . .